Feral Flesh

A Mystery/Suspense Short Story

David Bridge

Merry Vale Publishing

Feral Flesh: A Short Story

MUSIC. OR JUSTICE.
LIFE. OR DEATH.

Upper Redmore Estate: a Victorian-era mansion, boasts thirty acres, thirteen bedrooms, and the largest glasshouse in the country. In the hope of keeping the Estate afloat in the twenty-first century and beyond, its aging owner, Baron Alberic "Albie" Hewston-Perthwright the Third maintains a skeleton staff and hosts a smorgasbord of paying guests.

Recording their latest album, Albie's current guests are metal band Feral Flesh.

After a stint in rehab, Feral Flesh bass player, Bearbark, is late joining the band on the Estate. He should be in his element in the Gothic mansion, dressed in his black leather trench coat, black jeans, a steel crucifix hanging from his neck. But he feels uneasy.

Unsure whether he should be here at all.

And what should be a revelatory reunion takes a dark turn when Bearbark hears what Feral Flesh have been recording without him. Soon he will be faced with a choice which will put his love of music, his love for his friends, his only family, to the ultimate test.

"Feral Flesh" is a mystery/suspense short story which was first published in the July/August 2020 issue of Ellery Queen Mystery Magazine.

In "Feral Flesh" a weary metal band strikes an uneasy arrangement with an eccentric British aristocrat. An arrangement which threatens to destroy them both.

Something felt off the moment Bearbark crossed the threshold.

He had never liked these country mansions and he didn't think Upper Redmore Estate was going to do anything to change his mind. All the same, he hoped the uneasiness was merely his reaction to the house itself and not something more sinister.

The air in the entrance hall smelled of limestone and old leather. Dust rose in golden clouds. The black-and-white marble tiles beneath his feet made him feel like a pawn on a chessboard. Although it was an unseasonably warm November day, it was colder inside than out. Over his shoulder, through the gigantic, iron-studded oak door he had left open on his heels, he heard the taxi tyres crunching back down the mile-long gravel driveway.

He was all alone now.

And he was really doing this.

The taxi driver had sighed when Bearbark had flagged him down at the train station and told him where he wanted to go. There would be no chance of the driver picking up a fare on his way back into town. As far as Bearbark could tell, the nearest settlement was Linloave Village which they had passed through about five miles back.

It couldn't have had a population of more than a hundred.

Bearbark breathed in deeply, trying to get used to the house.

But it was like putting on a pair of shoes that was a size too big.

Being a metal guy, he should've relished a place like this. Redmore was a Victorian-era mansion; it boasted thirty acres, thirteen bedrooms, and the largest glasshouse in the country. What was more it had that Gothic aesthetic all his favourite bands borrowed from.

That his own band — Feral Flesh — borrowed from.

Bearbark imagined that to an observer he would have looked in his element here. He was dressed in a black shirt, black jeans. A steel crucifix hung from his neck, emerging from his thicket of curly black hair, the split ends brushing his abdomen. His leather trench coat swept the cuffs of his ankle boots as he clutched his bass guitar case at his right thigh; his duffle bag dangling down at his left.

"Beerbark?"

Bearbark's heart throbbed in his throat. He strained his neck to look.

There was a staircase ahead.

Someone had called down to him from there.

Now he heard footsteps, creaking floorboards.

Two suits of armour stood guard before him. One on either side of the staircase. Both bore spears and looked as if they might lurch to life at any moment, striding forward with a shriek of metal on metal, ready to strike down intruders.

A man with wild white hair popped into view, descending the staircase. He was wearing a baggy tracksuit that looked like a relic from the nineties. He was beanpole thin. His body shape, coupled with the fact that he stood on higher ground, made it feel as though he was a giant. As if aware of this effect and wanting to press its advantage, the man came to a halt three or four steps before the bottom of the staircase, clutching the rosewood banister.

A smile stitched back his lips. "Beerbark," he repeated.

"Bear-bark," Bearbark corrected him.

The man slapped his forehead and his smile transformed into a grimace. "Oh dear. My apologies, my apologies, Mister ... uh, Bearbark." He steadied himself a moment longer with the banister and the easy expression he had worn before returned. "Bearbark. Bearbark. I would ask whether you were Christened that ... but, well, it sounds rather pagan, doesn't it?"

"My parents named me Rory Horn."

"Ah-ha, I see," the man replied, and then descended the last few steps so they stood on level ground. The man was still a smudge taller than Bearbark. He stuck out his hand. "Baron Alberic Hewston-Perthwright the Third."

Just as Bearbark was about to clasp his palm, the man withdrew his hand.

Shaking his head, the man scolded himself. His tone of voice was too quiet for Bearbark to make out precisely what he said but he seemed to be telling himself off.

There were even a few swearwords thrown into the self-castigation.

There was an awkward pause and then the man recovered, pinning on the same smile as before. He extended his hand again for Bearbark to shake. "Please call me Albie," he said. "Yes, that would be much more appropriate." The man — Albie — scoffed at himself. "Really, you must think me quite the ninny for putting on such a show!"

Bearbark accepted Albie's hand. His skin was strangely cool and its texture reminded him of tree bark. When he had first seen Albie, he had thought he had been in his late-fifties, but now that he had got closer he wondered if he was wrong.

Was he seventy?

Eighty?

... Older?

Off in the distance of the house, Bearbark heard several dull echoes of what sounded like a snare drum being struck. That would be the rest of Feral Flesh. He yearned to go join them, to leave this strange man's company. It had been a long time since they had last seen one another. And a lot had changed since then.

"I was wondering ... why didn't you arrive with the rest of the band? They all got here about a week ago." His smile sharpened a shade or two. "They really do make an awful racket!"

Bearbark's chest tightened and his stomach sank. He hadn't risked any breakfast this morning. It was strange but he felt nervous. Even though his bandmates were his friends — his best friends — he felt as though they would need to get to know one another all over again. Although Bearbark had gone through hour after hour of therapy while in rehab, he still couldn't help but feel as though he was a burden to others.

Had been coming here a great mistake?

In rehab so much emphasis had been put upon breaking old patterns. On leaving behind old friends that served only self-destructive behaviour. But to leave his friends would have been to also leave behind the chance of making a living doing the one thing he loved.

It might've been different if Bearbark had instigated contact himself, but the band had been the ones to get in touch. They had sent him a letter.

If it hadn't been for that letter ...

The letter — the knowledge that they were all waiting for him — had given him the strength to get through those final days of rehab. And he hoped it would also give him the strength to stay sober in the face of temptation.

Feral Flesh was more than any of them.

And Bearbark had pledged to himself that he would protect it.

He shifted his attention back onto Albie who looked a touch sheepish now.

"I say, old chap, are you all right? I'm ever so sorry. I didn't mean to offend."

"It's fine — don't worry," Bearbark replied. "It was the plan all along."

"It was none of my business. I ..." His gaze focused upon Bearbark's left cheek.

Bearbark instinctively reached for the spot.

It was wet.

A tear had snaked down his face.

He wiped it away as though smushing a fly.

"Show you to your room?"

Although Bearbark wanted nothing more than to go and see his bandmates, he felt obliged to have Albie show him the room where he would be staying.

This was his house, after all.

This situation was akin to staying with a distant elderly relative. And although Bearbark hadn't seen his own family for the best part of a decade, he was unable to shake the urge to be polite. He had to indulge the old man for a little while.

The room itself was larger than the house Bearbark had grown up in.

Calling it a "room" was doing it a disservice.

It was more like a suite.

The suite was positioned in the top corner of what Albie explained was the East Wing. Albie had gone on to explain how lucky Bearbark was; that he would be the first in the house to get the rays of morning sun. Bearbark didn't think to point out that he had always been a night owl and that he had no intention of waking up any time before midday.

Let alone seeing the "morning sun".

To tell the truth, Bearbark was surprised Albie hadn't cottoned onto this likelihood after spending a week with his bandmates. None of them looked like the sort of people who were up with the lark.

The suite comprised a master bedroom, a lounging area, a bathroom, and a fully-stocked kitchenette. The master bedroom featured a four-poster bed complete with a velvet canopy and matching drapes the colour of scarlet. Bearbark dropped his duffle bag on top of the bed, holding onto his bass guitar case for the time being. The wallpaper was an off-white colour with flowery designs stencilled on in gold ink. There were also several oil paintings hanging on the bedroom walls. These featured what Bearbark thought of as traditional outdoor leisure pursuits of the English upper classes:

Fox-hunting, pheasant-shooting, fly-fishing, etcetera, etcetera.

Albie took great pleasure in drawing Bearbark's attention to the large window which allowed a view out across the grounds.

Bearbark examined the view, seeing that the whole Redmore Estate was surrounded by thick forest. On the taxi ride here he remembered thinking to himself that the trees seemed never ending. They were mostly elm trees, including what he had thought might be a wych elm. He might investigate further if he got the chance. At one point, when he was still at school, he had harboured dreams of going on to study botany. But then had come the drink, the drugs and the music and any thoughts of academic progress had been lost.

At the edge of the horizon, he thought he could just make out the spire of Linloave Village Church, peeping up over the canopy. Closer by, over to the western side of the estate, the wild-growing lawn sloped into a lake. Sunlight sparkled off the surface of the water.

It was difficult to believe that people really lived like this.

That people like this still actually existed.

"Shall I take you to see the others?" Albie asked. "Or would you like to rest a while?"

Bearbark lost himself, staring at the surface of the lake for the longest time.

It was easy to lose yourself in nature if you tried.

There was always something more to see.

Albie sidled up alongside him and Bearbark could tell that he was following his gaze, trying to see what he was looking at. "Is something the matter?" Albie asked, finally.

Bearbark tore his attention away from the window.

Put the lake out of his mind.

He summoned a half-smile from somewhere.

"No," he said. "It's nothing. I just ... it's a beautiful place, isn't it?"

A smile tweaked the corner of Albie's mouth. "The most wonderful place on Earth."

When Bearbark caught sight of the first mic stand he felt his face flush and he started to sweat. It was warmer in this part of the house, although physical warmth had little to do with the sensation he was experiencing. All the same, he would ditch his trench coat over the back of a chair once he'd got shot of Albie, who was lingering on his heels.

Bearbark took stock of the pop-up recording studio before him.

Oli's drum kit.

Warrick and Hakim's amplifier stacks.

Banks of guitars slotted into a wooden frame.

Mixing desk, computer screens ...

Cables snaking all over the floor.

A thrill passed through his gut.

"Servants' quarters, this," Albie said, his tone deadpan. "Or it was until the estate could no longer afford a full house staff." He sighed heavily. "I keep a skeleton crew these days but this would have been where they had their meals, and so on and so forth. That would have been during my grandfather's generation. Sad to think that so many good men and women were let go. Whole families moved through this house. A shame, really, that for the last ones their children would never have the opportunity to follow in their parents' footsteps.

They would never get the chance to add their own thread to Redmore's rich tapestry."

There being no sign of his bandmates, Bearbark rested his bass guitar case against the wall and took stock of the room itself.

There was an arching ceiling overhead and the floorboards were more worn here than in the rest of the house. There was also a notable lack of ornamentation. Everything here was functional. And why wouldn't it be? For these people, servants were part of the house itself.

Inanimate objects.

Or — as Albie had so neatly put it — "threads" in a tapestry.

Bearbark supposed dozens of servants had lived here, all squashed up together.

Across the room, he saw a wooden board with rows of bells nailed onto it. He had seen enough documentaries about these old houses to know that each one of those bells corresponded to a room in the house. When the bell rang a member of the house staff was expected to come running to indulge the noble's latest whim.

Albie went on, returning Bearbark to the present, "I did tell the boys they were welcome to set up in the ballroom but that curious blond-haired chap didn't seem to like the idea. Something about the 'acoustics'." He rolled his eyes. "I don't believe any of the musicians who played there throughout the centuries ever came across such a problem ... still, it's the 'modern way', I suppose."

Bearbark's ears perked up. "Blond-haired? You mean Emil?"

Emil was Feral Flesh's producer and sound engineer.

He was responsible for the layout before them.

"Yes, Scando chap?"

"He's Norwegian, yeah," Bearbark replied.

However, as he spoke, Emil himself appeared, framed in one of the many doorways leading into the hall.

Although it had been six months, Emil looked just how he remembered.

He was wearing a white denim jacket over a tattered black t-shirt and a pair of ripped blue jeans. His blond hair hung in neat curtains either side of his face.

Bearbark's stomach churned.

Emil grinned and threw his arms wide in celebration. He approached with his familiar limp — an injury inflicted while in his teens and working as a roadie back home in his native Norway. He had come to England shortly after to work as a junior engineer in night clubs and concert venues. "It's wonderful to see you, BB," Emil said, embracing Bearbark. "We're just so glad that you're here."

Although Bearbark was a clear head and shoulders taller than Emil, it was nice to have someone consoling him. Even if — like Emil — that person only rose to chest height.

During his time in rehab, it had become difficult to separate reality from fantasy in his mind's eye. He had been cautious whenever dealing with the memories which came to him while he lay awake on his bed at night, waiting to doze off. The substances he'd been taking had affected him so that he knew he was an unreliable witness to his own history. Whenever he'd turned those memories over in rehab, they had been fraught with paranoia, with a sense that the whole world was against him. Only now — now that he was sober and he'd had some time apart from the band — did he feel the love they had for him.

This was his family.

When they broke apart, Bearbark felt heat rising to his cheeks again. His eyes becoming watery. He turned his head away from Emil. "Sorry," he said, sniffing a laugh. "Not very metal, huh?"

Emil clapped him twice on the shoulder. "No worries, big man. You've been through a lot. We understand. Now we've got you back for good."

Bearbark glanced about. Albie had disappeared. "Where's he gone?" Bearbark asked.

Emil looked around too. He widened his eyes, stuck out his bottom lip and shrugged. "That guy's a force of nature. He pops up just when you're least expecting it — disappears whenever you get used to having him around. He spends a good amount of the day just running circles around the grounds."

"Is he crazy?"

"What, like a hamster in a wheel? That sort of thing? Perhaps. But what're you gonna do?" Emil broke into another grin. "It's so great to have you back, bro. I'm telling you, you're gonna love this place. We've got so much work done here. It's just so ... so ..."

"Tranquil?" Bearbark volunteered.

"Yeah, yeah. But it's also ... oh, man, this house is just awesome. Just wait till you see the breakfasts Ms Agatha puts on — she's Albie's housekeeper. And, shit, man" — he was nearly in hysterics now — "we went for a walk out in the woods the other day. We took a wrong turn somewhere. I thought we were gonna die out there. Don't know how we didn't. Just lucky, I guess."

Bearbark smiled faintly. "Sounds like you've had a great time."

"And the rooms, man! I've got this bath I could have a threesome in." He paused. "Not that I've had a chance to give it a try out here." He bowed his head in mock apology. "Sorry to disappoint, but dudes with long hair who dress in black have never really done it for me. And that's all that seems to be going around here."

Bearbark picked up the slack. "We're really in the middle of nowhere here, huh?"

"Yeah!" Emil replied. "That's what's got us so productive, man. I mean, we must've got like thirty rough tracks down just this week ... oh, hell, come over and I'll show you."

Bearbark got the uncomfortable, itchy sensation that someone was watching him. He checked over his shoulder. There was nobody there.

He followed Emil.

After about forty minutes sat at the computer screen, listening through the studio monitors to a selection of recordings Feral Flesh had made in the last week, Bearbark recalled the drawback to Emil's constant energy. It could be draining. He had forgotten that he didn't have an off switch. The only remedy was to interrupt otherwise Emil could easily talk all day.

And all night.

When Emil reached the end of the current track — something that was tentatively titled "Blood Bane" — Bearbark spoke up.

"Before we meet the others," Bearbark said, "I just wanted to thank you for filling in for me. In rehab, I thought about it a lot and I know that it would've been so much harder going facing up to my shit knowing that I'd bumped the rest of the guys off the road."

Although more of a studio guy, when the time had come for Bearbark to check himself into rehab, the label had arranged for Emil to fill in on bass for the rest of the tour. It made sense. Even though he rarely played with the band live, in practice Emil was the de facto fifth member of the group. He even had songwriting credits in addition to his production on their first record. And — from what Bearbark had listened to so far — it looked as though he would get those same credits on this record too.

"Aw, man, don't start with that soppy shit, okay? You know I got paid for it. That's thanks enough. It was just a job."

Bearbark wasn't sure when Emil had decided that life on the road wasn't for him, but he couldn't help thinking that it was the smartest decision he might've made. If someone like Bearbark — who had always considered himself to be reserved, bordering on withdrawn, in social situations — could get himself into a tangle with all the shenanigans on the road then someone with Emil's get-up-and-go personality might well end up dead in six months.

Luckily, it had only been a handful of shows.

In the studio, Emil could constructively channel the more obsessive traits of his personality into the music.

Emil breathed in deeply, squared his shoulders, straightened his back. This was a pose Bearbark knew well. It was the pose that Emil struck whenever he had something borderline serious that he felt needed to be expressed. "You know I'll step back now, huh? All that bass you hear on these tracks, they're just a guide. I wanna hear your take on it, okay?" There was another spark in Emil's eye and Bearbark knew that he was about to be carried away on a verbal tsunami again. Emil grinned. "Can I play you just this one track? It's called 'Shot Down in a Hurricane' ... oh, man, your playing's gonna sound fucking amazing on this."

Even though Bearbark knew Emil was just indulging his ego by saying they were going to rerecord the songs with Bearbark playing, it touched him deeply. From his dealings with other bands out on tour, he couldn't help feeling that Feral Flesh operated in a far more harmonious manner than was normal.

Everyone got a say.

And everyone was listened to.

There was no room for bullshit.

And yet ... Bearbark had nearly fucked it all up.

"Who's this tosser then?!"

Bearbark nearly upturned the cup of coffee Emil had brought to him about twenty minutes ago. The coffee was now stone cold and Bearbark set the cup aside so that it was no longer in danger from flying elbows.

He pivoted in the chair, away from the computer screen, where Emil had left him to listen to more of the music Feral Flesh had put down in the last week. They had been doing about six hours of recorded jams a day so there was well over thirty hours to wade through.

Thirty hours for Bearbark to catch up on.

Warrick stood slightly ahead of Oli and Hakim, the three of them forming a loose triangular formation. There was something defensive Bearbark detected about the posture, as if Oli and Hakim were hanging back. Perhaps they were afraid he might explode.

Although Bearbark liked to think there was a refreshing lack of ego surrounding Feral Flesh, there was no doubt about who the leader of the group was.

Warrick had cut the sides of his hair short since Bearbark had last seen him, slicking what remained into a sharp arrowhead down his back. He wore a waist-high leather jacket over his bare torso. Warrick had always said that he liked the feeling of "flesh on flesh".

The tattoo of an osprey across his chest was a new acquisition.

Feeling a touch giddy now — everything seemed to be happening very quickly all of a sudden — Bearbark rose from the chair. After Emil had brought him his coffee, he had slipped out to go and make a phone call to the label.

Warrick gave Bearbark an arm wrestle-style handshake and they bumped shoulders.

Oli and Hakim followed.

They hadn't changed anything about themselves at all.

Like Bearbark, they still both had long, flowing black hair and were dressed in the same clothes they'd worn six months ago out on tour.

"Good to see you, man," Oli said.

And then Hakim, "Great to have you back."

Once the greetings were over and done with there was a slightly uncomfortable pause.

Thankfully, Warrick broke it without too much delay.

"We just got back from taking a stroll around the grounds. You're gonna love it here. I can't remember anything like it." Warrick nodded to the computer. "Been listening to what we've been up to?"

For some strange reason, Bearbark felt a shade embarrassed, as if by listening to what his bandmates had been up to without him was something shameful. As if he should've asked them permission rather than Emil.

But he knew he was being ridiculous.

Feral Flesh was his band ... until the others kicked him out.

"It's sounding good," Bearbark said. "I mean, I'm looking forward to working on the ideas you've been getting down."

Warrick exchanged glances with Oli and Hakim.

Bearbark couldn't help but feel that there was something afoot.

When Warrick spoke it was something of a relief. "We've been thinking," Warrick said. "It's been going so well here, things have just been flowing ... this could be a double."

Bearbark's head was spinning. "A double album?"

Warrick looked to Oli and Hakim again, as if this was something that they had already agreed among themselves. For all that Bearbark knew, they had. "Yeah, I think Emil's speaking with the label right now about it, actually. But as long as they clear it, I reckon that's the direction we're headed ..."

Another lengthy silence.

"You think we've got the clout?" Bearbark asked.

Warrick gave a sheepish grin, coupled with a shrug. "Emil seems to think so and you know how much time he spends with that lot — he's with them every day. He has a good read on them."

Bearbark breathed in deeply once more.

Was he getting more used to the house, or was it becoming stranger?

He surprised himself when he started to speak. "The first record ... the first one ... it took us eighteen months to get those songs in order, to get it all ready. And then it was a week in the studio. All done. This time ..."

"It's just different," Warrick put in, finishing Bearbark's sentence for him. "It's like all the other bands on the road we talked to were saying. Once you're on the treadmill you've gotta keep on walking otherwise the ground gets pulled out from under your feet. It's like they say. Write. Record. Tour."

"Repeat," Bearbark added.

Warrick snorted a laugh. "Yeah. Until we get bored or one of us has a kid or whatever."

Although the others raised a smile at this, Bearbark couldn't help but sense that there was some uncomfortable truth to what Warrick said.

And they would all have to confront it sooner or later.

Dinner that night was nothing short of spectacular.

And Ms Agatha hadn't turned out to be the world-weary widow Bearbark had expected. No, in contrast to her Gothic surroundings, she was jovial, joking with the others as she served thick tenderloin steaks and fries she had prepared in Bearbark's honour (they had told her that it was one of his favourite dishes, and they were not mistaken). For dessert, they had had a chocolate mousse (another of Bearbark's favourites). While the others had decided they were going to watch a film in the basement cinema, Bearbark had felt on edge; a sort of guilt, perhaps. He was aware of how much work there was to do.

And a double album.

That afternoon, Emil had informed them that the label had agreed in principle to the idea. The final decision would be down to the band. And while the others were in favour, Bearbark knew he had to listen to what they had come up with to be sure.

Everything was happening too fast.

And Bearbark was already so behind.

While the others disappeared off to the basement cinema, Bearbark retreated to the studio, taking up his place in front of the computer monitor, snapping a pair of headphones on over his ears. Instantly, he slipped into the calm of the throbbing rhythms.

This was what he had most missed while in rehab.

Not the booze, not the drugs ... but the music.

After about ten minutes, he unclasped his guitar case and slipped out his sable-black bass. This was the first time he had actually held the instrument since he had got out of rehab. When his property had been returned to him, he hadn't so much as glimpsed inside the case that'd been handed back. Although it sounded ridiculous, he had felt that some kind of monster might slip out, slash him across the throat.

That same monster which'd put him in rehab in the first place.

Now, though — now, it was different.

As Bearbark listened to the layered riffs fizzling through his eardrums, he channelled into Emil's bassline. He was a skilled player, of that there was no doubt, but he was also so correct. So in the pocket, each and every time. He stood out.

At least in Feral Flesh.

They all sounded loose by comparison.

It was as if Emil was setting the rhythm when it should've been Oli on the drums. As if he was slipping the band into melody when it should've been Hakim's lead guitar lines. As if he was pushing the dynamics when it should've been Warrick's vocals.

Bearbark closed his eyes, listening to his bandmates thrash on and on around Emil's staunch foundation. He fingered the fretboard, imagining his bandmates playing around him in his mind. As he stepped all over Emil's basslines, he realised Emil hadn't been trying to "manage" him by saying they wanted Bearbark to rerecord the tracks with his own playing.

It was actually something Bearbark supposed he had believed all along.

Deep down.

He was an essential part of Feral Flesh's sound.

And they needed him.

Bearbark guessed he must've played for hours, alone in the servants' quarters. He hadn't played for so long that he had lost the callouses on his fingertips. Even though he would've played on all night if he'd been able, the pain in his fingers forced him to stop around one a.m. Although he replaced his bass in its case, he remained in the chair, perusing the recordings, knowing there was still so much for him to hear.

Emil had already started off the process of organising the raw recording sessions. He had cut up the jams and given them names so it would be easier to check them over later. Feeling somewhat overwhelmed by the quantity awaiting, Bearbark skimmed the titles with his mouse cursor, eventually coming to a recording titled, "Laid to Rest in the Lake".

He hit play.

At first, Bearbark thought he hadn't clicked the filename.

There was no sound.

Or so it seemed.

After about ten seconds, and as Bearbark readied to click onto the next recording in the list, he heard a whisper in his headphones.

"... Laid ... them down ... in the lake ... they rest ... in the lake ... in the water ... laid them down ..."

Bearbark's heart tapped at the roof of his mouth.

A tingling sensation ran up his spine.

He hit pause.

Pulled the headphones off his head and laid them on the table.

He blinked out into the surrounding darkness of the servants' quarters.

There was nobody there.

It was just him.

He glanced back at the computer monitor.

He had reached the end of the recording and he could hear the hiss and fuzz of the next session crackling out of the headphones.

Perhaps it was time for bed.

It had been a long day.

He could call it a night.

Bearbark shut down the computer, headed out of the servants' quarters.

It was only when he slipped in under his bedsheets that he admitted to himself that it had been Albie's voice he had heard on that recording.

But why?

Although Bearbark initially tossed and turned while trying to get to sleep, once he finally did go under he didn't surface until well after midday. When he rose, trod over to the window to look out over the estate, he saw it was overcast, chillier than yesterday.

A more typical November day.

It appeared that the house was allowing for the sleeping habits of its guests after all.

The kitchen was still serving breakfast when Bearbark went down.

In fact, Emil was still eating when he arrived.

The breakfast room had large windows which looked out over the verdant lawns and onto the lake at the foot of the hill. There was a long bench which had been covered with a white tablecloth, a place still set for Bearbark.

Thankfully, it didn't seem that Albie was present.

Perhaps he was jogging around the grounds, as Emil had suggested yesterday.

Fork thrust in the air, spearing a half sausage, Emil gave Bearbark a welcoming smile, speaking through his mouthful. "Looks like I wasn't the only one up late last night."

Bearbark took the place set for him at the table.

"Sleep well?"

"Yeah. A little too well, I guess."

Soon Bearbark saw first-hand what Emil had meant about Ms Agatha's breakfasts.

It was a full English breakfast: bacon, sausages, eggs, black pudding, baked beans, fried tomatoes and mushrooms along with slices of wholemeal toast, pots of tea and coffee.

Bearbark could never have been accused of a lack of appetite and today was no exception. Even despite what he had on his mind — what had been on his mind since the previous evening.

Bearbark greeted Ms Agatha. She wore a pinafore apron and treated him to a rosy-cheeked smile. She laid his breakfast plate on the table before him, patting him on the shoulder affectionately on her way back to the kitchen.

Bearbark couldn't recall the last time he had been on the receiving end of anything approaching motherly affection. Perhaps back when he'd been a teenager and gone to visit a friend's house. That had always baffled him about mothers — at least other people's mothers — how they treated other children as if they were surrogates.

As if they were precious just for existing.

Just for being children.

All the same, motherly attentions or not, Bearbark made sure that Ms Agatha was out of earshot before he shared his misgivings with Emil.

"Last night I was listening to the recordings," Bearbark said.

Emil eyed Bearbark over the rim of his coffee cup.

"I ... it all sounds great ... but I wanted to ask about one of them ... something that, I don't know ... it just doesn't seem to fit ..."

Emil sipped at his coffee, then set the cup down. "We've got so much material we're going to have to cut ruthlessly. Even if it does end up being a double."

"Yeah, I understand that," Bearbark said. "I was more interested in where one of the recordings came from." He met Emil's eye. "How the recording came about."

"Okay."

"It was called 'Laid in the Lake', something like that?"

" 'Laid to Rest in the Lake' ?"

Again Bearbark had the uncomfortable feeling that he was being watched.

He looked around ... and could find no likely observer.

Still, that didn't mean someone wasn't there.

"It sounds like Albie," Bearbark added.

More than anything, Bearbark wanted Emil to break out into one of his familiar snarky grins. Or to make some sort of a quip. That would've laid his fears to rest.

But Emil remained expressionless.

And it put Bearbark further on edge.

"I left the mics on one evening," Emil said, "when we went to have dinner. I wanted to get a bit of ambience from the house. Draughts blowing through, creaky floorboards, water washing through pipes, that sort of thing, you know?" He pressed his lips together so tightly that he squeezed the blood from them. When he spoke again, he dropped his voice so that it was a raspy whisper. "But when we came back, well ... you heard it for yourself."

Bearbark felt his muscles tauten. "Did you think what it might mean?"

Ms Agatha emerging from the kitchen distracted Emil's attention.

"Can I get you gentlemen anything else?" she asked.

A plan was set for the band to meet up at four; that they would play together for the first time since Bearbark's return. Although Bearbark should have been a bag of nerves at the prospect of playing with the band for the first time in six months, there was something else on his mind: "Laid to Rest in the Lake".

There was only a single spot in his room where Bearbark could get signal on his smartphone. When he did, he did an internet search on Redmore, hoping that it might turn something up. He found a potted history of the estate, and then an article which featured a much younger Albie meeting the Queen.

It was the news item towards the end of the search which drew his attention, though.

"Week-long search abandoned at Redmore Estate"

Bearbark clicked the link and went through to the article.

He skimmed the text quickly, moving so fast that every five or six words he had to force himself to run back and make sure he had read the details correctly.

It concerned Baron Hewston-Perthwright — Albie's — wife and daughter who had both one day seemingly gone out into the woods and failed to return. There was a brief interview with Albie, who had been brought into police custody for questioning, and then there was also mention of Ms Agatha, who had been called upon to give a statement. The article concluded that the disappearance of Albie's wife and daughter had been unresolved and that in the absence of any further evidence the case against Albie was to be dropped.

Bearbark looked up, peered through the window, and down to the lake.

Bearbark was unsure about what he hoped to achieve by stepping out onto the grounds. His head was spinning, though, and the only way to let off the excess energy seemed to be to take some sort of exercise.

The chill was greater than he had anticipated. He turned up the collar of his trench coat. Although his boots hadn't ventured too far from urban environs, their deep treads were standing him in good stead now, gripping the slanting damp earth beneath his soles, stopping him from slipping as he descended the slope down to the lake.

His heart pounded in his ears in a way that mimicked the sensation he experienced whenever on the brink of succumbing to a cold.

When he reached the water, he felt the chill of the air rising up from the surface.

He stared down into the gritty, grey depths.

What did he think he might see down there?

... Who did he think he might see down there?

Was there any doubt?

Not to his mind ...

"I trust you had a good rest."

Albie's voice sent a shudder through Bearbark.

Bearbark glanced up.

Saw Albie standing before him.

He wore the same tracksuit he had had on the day before. Perspiration sparkled on his brow. He was slightly out of breath which suggested he had been running.

Had he seen Bearbark and come running?

And then Bearbark's eyes drifted to what Albie held down at his side.

A hatchet.

The kind that might be used to hack kindling.

His whole body froze.

Bearbark knew he could run ... Albie might have been half a century older than he was ... surely he could outrun him if it came to that.

But doubt nagged at his mind.

If Albie came at him suddenly Bearbark knew it might all be over.

Albie peered at the water out of the corner of his eye, as if afraid to trust it completely. It concealed secrets, after all. "It seems another lifetime ago, now," Albie said. "It will be forty years this summer."

"Forty years from what?" Bearbark asked.

Albie snapped away from the water, his eyes lingering over Bearbark. It was then that a new expression — one which Bearbark hadn't previously seen — crossed Albie's face.

A sneer.

"Don't lie, please. We understand one another. Shall we settle on that?"

Bearbark eyed the hatchet Albie held down at his side, seeing he was gripping it so tightly that his knuckles had turned white. Bearbark sensed movement out of the corner of his eye. Although it went against his better judgement, he couldn't help but glance up the hill, back towards the house.

He saw four figures approaching.

Gradually descending the hill just as he had done.

Feral Flesh.

His band.

Bearbark had a long time to think through his possible courses of action as they approached. The most obvious was to make a break for the woods ... was that what Albie's wife and daughter had attempted?

But there were five of them ... and only one of him ...

Until the search arrived.

It was then that he realised just how alone in the world he really was. He hadn't told anybody he had come here. Nobody outside the band — outside the label — had even known that he had checked into rehab. He had no home. No neighbours.

No family.

Nobody to miss him.

Somehow he had become the perfect murder victim.

A man with no ties.

Just as it had been yesterday when Bearbark had reunited with the group, Warrick was the one to lead the others. All of their expressions were stone, seemingly devoid of emotion. Warrick flashed a glance at the lake as if in silent acknowledgement of the truth they all knew. Bearbark's eyes found Emil's ... although he glanced away quickly.

Albie began to speak. "They wanted to leave Redmore ..." He shook his head, trembling now, the hatchet nearly dropping from his quivering grip. "But I couldn't allow that ... I ... didn't believe I was capable ... I don't believe even they believed I was capable ... they didn't even scream. Not even my daughter."

Oppressive, slate-grey clouds dangled above their heads.

Bearbark shifted away from Albie. It was important he heard what his band had to say. What they had to say through Warrick, their conduit.

"We made a deal," Warrick said.

"All charges waived," Albie said, in a dead tone.

"The label are happy," Warrick went on, "and we're making the best music of our career. Perhaps it's ... maybe we're really channelling ... you know, something? The music we make. So many other groups sound so ... so forced. You scratch the surface and it's all a paintjob, you know? Maybe we've found something genuine. Pure inspiration, if you like."

Bearbark felt as though the world had become squashy beneath his feet.

Again, he had the urge to retreat.

But at the same time he knew it would be in vain.

"Do the label know everything?" Bearbark asked.

This time Emil chipped in. "Not everything. Of course not. What we all know cannot leave those of us standing here. All I can say is that they think what I've sent them so far is promising. More than promising — it could be something great."

Bearbark didn't appreciate the vaguely bragging tone Emil struck.

It wasn't appropriate.

Not in the slightest.

"We can keep coming back," Warrick said, picking up where Emil left off. "Just think about it ... if we keep this inspiration alive who knows what we're capable of? This is the rest of our lives. Right here."

Bearbark felt his chest tighten.

His gut dropped.

"The rest of our lives", that phrase echoed about his skull.

What about Albie's wife and daughter?

What about the rest of their lives?

Finally, Bearbark glanced up, unable to prevent himself looking at the hatchet as he did so. "Do I have a choice?" he asked.

Nobody replied to his question.

Because no answer was necessary.

The driving bass drum throbbed through Bearbark.

His fingers slithered up and down the fretboard, his natural sense of rhythm and phrasing ebbing in and out of Oli's rudiments. Together, they provided the steady canvas on which Warrick and Hakim painted riff, melody, as they gave life to Feral Flesh.

Although Bearbark was aware of the others around him, the headphones clasped over his ears made it seem as though he occupied his own private jail cell. As if he was in company but trapped ... condemned to forever be alone.

Condemned.

As Bearbark reached the summit of the latest rushing phrase, and allowed his fingers to fall back into the simmering rhythm, he glanced over at Emil, manning the sound desk. He was hunched over the knobs, dials and sliders, mesmerised by the mix running through his own headphones. For a fraction of a second, he met Bearbark's eye.

Something passed between them.

A spark?

... Or was that too cliché?

As if the band — as one and separate from Bearbark — had conspired to draw his attention elsewhere, Oli fired off a drumroll, Hakim performed a run up the fretboard while Warrick gave a deep-throated battle cry.

It was the sequence that Bearbark knew would lead into "Laid to Rest in the Lake".

Halfway through the song, the thrashing noise would subside, leaving only Baron Alberic Hewston-Perthwright the Third's quiet ramblings. His admission to the murders he had committed. It was almost as if they had acquired a sixth band member.

Before, playing with Feral Flesh had never failed to move Bearbark. Now, though, it was different. Things would never be the same. When they eventually left Redmore Estate Bearbark knew a choice awaited him; one which would once again throw his entire world up in the air:

Music.

Or justice.

Life.

Or death.

He had to decide.

Author's Note

Thank you for taking the time to read "Feral Flesh", I really hope you enjoyed reading it as much as I enjoyed writing it!

This story is special to me as it was the first one I had published professionally (in the July/August 2020 issue of Ellery Queen Mystery Magazine).

If you would like to get in touch with me by email you can do so at: hello@davidiainbridge.com

Sign up for my newsletter and hear about all my latest releases and promotions at: www.davidiainbridge.com

Thanks for reading!

David

www.ingramcontent.com/pod-product-compliance
Lightning Source LLC
Chambersburg PA
CBHW020946160726
47993CB00007B/2955